Caroline Evensen Lazo

Twenty-First Century Books
Minneapolis

To Tyler, Chloe, and Cory

Acknowledgements: Special thanks to Lyndel King, Doreen Nelson, Penny and David Winton, and Gehry Partners, LLP, for their kindness in participating in this project

A&E and **BIOGRAPHY** are trademarks of A&E Television Networks. All rights reserved.

Some of the people profiled in this series have also been featured in the acclaimed BIOGRAPHY® series, on A&E Network, which is available on videocassette from A&E Home Video.

Text copyright © 2006 by Caroline Evensen Lazo

All rights reserved. International copyright secured. No part of this book may be reproduced, stored in a retrieval system, or transmitted in any form or by any means—electronic, mechanical, photocopying, recording, or otherwise—without the prior written permission of Lerner Publishing Group, except for the inclusion of brief quotations in an acknowledged review.

Twenty-First Century Books
A division of Lerner Publishing Group
241 First Avenue North
Minneapolis, MN 55401 U.S.A.

Website address: www.lernerbooks.com

Library of Congress Cataloging-in-Publication Data

Lazo, Caroline Evensen.
   Frank Gehry / by Caroline Evensen Lazo.
     p.   cm. — (A&E biography)
   Includes bibliographical references and index.
   ISBN-13: 978–0–8225–2649–0 (lib. bdg. : alk. paper)
   ISBN-10: 0–8225–2649–2 (lib. bdg. : alk. paper)
   1. Gehry, Frank O., 1929—Juvenile literature. 2. Architects—United States—Juvenile literature. I. Title. II. A&E biography (Twenty-First Century Books (Firm))
NA737.G44L39 2006
725'.092—dc22   2005002903

Manufactured in the United States of America
1 2 3 4 5 6 – BP – 11 10 09 08 07 06

Contents

1. Opening Night 7
2. Early Memories 11
3. Why Not Architecture? 19
4. "I'm Not Weird" 27
5. Imaginings 39
6. The Art of Architecture 53
7. "Swoopy" in Seattle 63
8. Miracle on First Street 69
9. The Biloxi Effect? 81
10. Back to the Future 91
    Epilogue 97
    Timeline 99
    Selected Buildings by Frank Gehry 101
    Buildings in Progress 102
    Sources 103
    Selected Bibliography 106
    Further Reading and Websites ... 108
    Index 109

Fireworks fly from the Walt Disney Concert Hall in Los Angeles, California, after the opening concert by the Los Angeles Philharmonic Orchestra on October 23, 2003.

Chapter **ONE**

OPENING NIGHT

ON OCTOBER 23, 2003, MUSIC LOVERS FROM around the world gathered in Los Angeles, California, for the opening of the Walt Disney Concert Hall. The concert hall was named after the world-famous cartoonist and filmmaker, but the star of the evening was the world-renowned architect Frank O. Gehry, who had designed the new building. Movie actors, business leaders, and government officials joined more than 2,250 others at the debut of Gehry's "musical pleasure palace," the new home of the Los Angeles Philharmonic Orchestra.

Lillian Disney, Walt Disney's widow, had initiated the project in memory of her husband's love of classical music and longtime association with the city of Los

Angeles. Also, her family gave the largest single gift toward financing the project. On opening night, the concert hall's glittering steel exterior lit up the landscape and stole the attention from the stars. Cameras clicked and flashed as dignitaries entered the building, and 350 members of the media broadcast the event around the world.

Gehry had won international fame when the stunning Guggenheim Museum in Bilbao, Spain, opened in 1997. Its swooping metal forms are familiar Gehry trademarks. He has won numerous awards for his work, which ranges from a bank headquarters in Berlin, Germany, to a rock-and-roll museum in Seattle, Washington. But his connection to the concert hall in Los Angeles is a more personal one. He had always wanted to design a building that would combine his love of music with his love of architecture in the city he had known since his youth. He wanted to show how architecture—the art of designing new spaces—could bring people together and lift their spirits.

Not everyone loved the new concert hall. One critic called it "half-torn-up cardboard boxes spray-painted silver." But Gehry is used to controversy. As a teenager, he learned how to deal with opposition and to triumph over it. Poverty and anti-Semitism haunted his early teens. Bullies beat him up because he was Jewish and teased him because he was small for his age. The strong support of his parents and grandparents guided him through those stormy days.

Frank was a shy young boy and spent much of his time alone. "I was the dreamer in the family when I was a kid," Gehry told the *New York Times*. Yet he never dreamed that one day he would design buildings with shiny exteriors that would light up whole towns or that he would become an international star.

The Talmud is one of the holy books of Judaism. It contains scholarly commentary on the sacred texts of Judaism.

Chapter **TWO**

EARLY MEMORIES

FRANK OWEN GEHRY WAS BORN FRANK OWEN Goldberg in Toronto, the capital of Ontario, Canada, in 1929. Frank's grandparents, Sam and Lillian Caplan Goldberg, had moved to Canada from Poland, where their Jewish heritage was deeply rooted. Sam Goldberg was a scholar who enjoyed discussing the teachings of the Talmud, the collection of ancient writings that forms the basis of Jewish law. Jewish traditions became a major part of Frank's home life in Canada.

The tradition that impressed Frank the most was one that his grandmother practiced weekly. Every Thursday she bought a live carp—a large freshwater fish—at Kensington Market in Toronto. She used the carp to make gefilte fish (balls or cakes of seasoned, minced fish) on Friday for the Jewish Sabbath. Between the time of the purchase and the time of preparation, she let the fish swim in her bathtub. The sight of a large fish in the bathtub startled and delighted young Frank. Watching the fish was fun, and Frank always looked forward to Thursdays at his grandparents' house.

Gehry's memories of fish later influenced his sculptures. This sculpture is located in the sculpture garden of the Walker Art Center in Minneapolis, Minnesota.

CREATIVE ADVENTURES

Frank's visits with his grandparents formed a variety of happy memories. He loved to play with building blocks, and his grandmother not only encouraged his creative activity but also joined in the fun. They played together for hours. "She was my model of how an adult can play creatively," he said. "We made houses, we made cities, it was wonderful." Caplan's Hardware, his grandparents' hardware store, also sparked his imagination. Frank learned about tools and building materials—wood, glass, metal, fencing—and loved to explore their functions.

He showed an early interest in art materials as well. His mother, Thelma Goldberg, took him to the Art Gallery of Ontario (AGO), the Royal Ontario Museum, and to symphony concerts at Toronto's Massey Hall. However, Frank's father, Irving Goldberg, called Frank a dreamer and thought his son wouldn't amount to anything.

But Irving Goldberg was somewhat of a dreamer himself. He was "something of a pop artist," Frank's younger sister Doreen remembered. Their father's creations—including an American flag made of fruits and vegetables and a papier-mâché horse, which was "light as a feather yet strong enough to stand on"—fascinated young Frank. He loved the idea of molding wet paper mixed with paste to make new shapes and forms. His father's ability to use ordinary materials to make extraordinary things enchanted him. Irving, a

Frank visited the Royal Ontario Museum in Toronto, Canada, when he was a child.

former boxer, also loved sports. But Frank was too small to participate in most sports. Instead, he liked to read magazines—*Popular Mechanics,* in particular— and enjoyed activities at the Young Men's Hebrew Association (YMHA).

When Frank entered the seventh grade, the Goldberg family moved to Timmins, a small mining town in Ontario, where Irving Goldberg started a business manufacturing and selling slot machines. Irving liked to move wherever he saw a better business opportunity. He liked to start new businesses. In Timmins Frank went into business too. He bought copies of the *Daily Press* newspaper at three cents each and sold them for five cents apiece. Though his business prospered, he faced problems at school.

Anti-Semitism began to plague young Frank. "I was the only Jewish kid at my school, and I was regularly beaten up for killing Christ... and [for some unknown reason] they called me Fish," he recalled. "I used to hear him cry," Doreen said.

The bullying at school prompted Frank to turn away from his Jewish roots, and he even began to question the existence of God. It was not unusual for bullies to prey on Jewish children—even in Canada. At that time, during World War II (1939–1945), Jews around the world were growing fearful. Millions were dying in Nazi death camps in Europe.

In the mid-1940s, the Canadian government made gambling illegal throughout Canada. That ended Irving Goldberg's slot machine business. The family moved back to Toronto, where Frank had his bar mitzvah (the ceremony that initiates a thirteen-year-old boy into adulthood) and entered Bloor Collegiate High School. His father invested in a furniture business.

Unexpected twists and turns seemed to characterize Irving's life after that, and he often kept his family on edge. Bad luck seemed to haunt him, and he constantly moved from one business to another. "He lost several fortunes and subjected the family to frightening cycles of boom and bust," Doreen remembered. And Frank recalled, "I felt very well off until I was thirteen or fourteen. Then we lost everything."

STARTING OVER

Finally, after he suffered a heart attack, Irving took his doctor's advice and made plans to move his family to a healthier climate. In 1947, soon after Frank's graduation from high school, Irving, Thelma, Frank, and Doreen moved to Los Angeles, California. But starting over was not easy. According to Doreen, "It was devastating."

The family moved into a small apartment near the downtown area. Thelma took care of her ailing husband, and she worked in a department store to support the family. She provided order and stability in her children's lives. "I had solutions to things," she told the *New York Times*. And she always found time to encourage Frank's interest in art. "She knew how to raise her children," Doreen said. "She was *with* us, she listened to us ... and encouraged creative play." To Frank and Doreen, she was "spectacular."

Because of the nine-year difference in their ages, Doreen and Frank spent little time together while growing up. When Frank was nineteen, Doreen was ten. But she still remembers the "brotherly things" he did for her. She enjoyed studying music, and she recalls Frank carrying her harp and loading it into the trunk of the car. "He was my hero," she said.

This aerial view of Los Angeles shows the campus of the University of Southern California as it was in the late 1990s. Gehry studied fine arts and architecture there as a young man.

Chapter **THREE**

WHY NOT ARCHITECTURE?

GEHRY'S PARENTS COULDN'T AFFORD FULL TUITION AT the University of Southern California (USC), so Frank took courses at night. To pay for evening art classes at USC, he worked for a company that made prefabricated, or partially assembled, kitchen eating areas, and he became a truck driver as well. Driving a large truck around town made him feel more adult, more in control. He liked that. And he liked to look at different parts of town and wonder what could be done to make them more attractive.

From 1949 to 1951, Gehry enrolled as a fine arts major at USC. He loved to transform objects and combine unlikely ones (as his father did when he created an American flag out of colorful fruits and vegetables). Minimalism (art that uses a few simple elements) made a lasting impression on him.

During one particular art class, a ceramics class, Gehry's teacher, Glen Lukens, sensed that Frank might have an interest in architecture. Lukens took Gehry to a construction site where Gehry saw architect Rafael Soriano more or less guiding construction. Gehry was fascinated by the architect's notes about the progress being made by construction workers. Gehry's art teacher was impressed by his keen interest in the building process and suggested he take some courses in architecture. Always open to new ideas, Gehry thought—why not? Soon afterward he enrolled in the architecture program at USC as a full-time student. He immediatley excelled and knew that he wanted to be an architect.

While working his way through college, Frank met Anita Snyder, and in 1952 the couple was married. They had two children, daughters Brina and Leslie. Anita urged her husband to change his Jewish surname to protect his children from the anti-Semitism that hurt him as a boy. He chose the name Gehry because it was different and it "also started with G." But as he told *Time* magazine, "I've always regretted changing [my name]."

In 1953 he spent a year as a designer of commercial spaces for Victor Gruen Associates in Los Angeles. With his wife's support, Gehry was able to earn his bachelor's degree in architecture at USC in 1954. After he completed his studies at USC, Gehry studied the giants of twentieth-century architecture—including Frank Lloyd Wright, Ludwig Mies Van Der Rohe, Walter Gropius, Le Corbusier, and Philip Johnson. They inspired Gehry. He spent the following year in the U.S. Army, Special Services Division. In 1956 the family moved to Cambridge, Massachusetts, where Gehry studied city planning at the Harvard Graduate School of Design. But the classes focused mainly on numbers and theories, and he soon lost interest. At an art exhibition in Cambridge, he saw the paintings of the Swiss-born French architect Le Corbusier, one of the most influential architects of the twentieth century. Le Corbusier's work delighted and intrigued him.

World-renowned architect Le Corbusier

The sweeping curves Le Corbusier used for the Notre-Dame-du-Haut chapel influenced Gehry's later designs.

Turning Points

Le Corbusier, who was also a sculptor, used graceful, sculpted forms in his architecture. The curving forms used in his Notre-Dame-du-Haut chapel in Ronchamp, France, appealed to Gehry. This freedom to use new shapes and forms inspired him to explore his own daring ideas regarding design and materials. Le Corbusier's chapel convinced Gehry that not every structure had to have straight angles or look "mechanistic." Not every new building had to look like a square box, which seemed to be the trend at the time.

Frank decided to return to Los Angeles. He worked for various firms before rejoining Victor Gruen Associates, where he was project director from 1958 to 1960. He spent the following year in Paris, working in the office of architect André Remondet. The next year, 1962, was a turning point for Gehry. His father died, and he established his own architectural firm, Frank O. Gehry & Associates, in Los Angeles. Like most architects, Gehry worked closely with his clients to fulfill their wishes. Unlike most architects, he dared to use inexpensive materials and ordinary objects in creative ways.

For example, in 1966 he constructed the little O'Neil Hay Barn in Orange County, California, with corrugated (folded or ridged) metal and telephone poles. It was the first of his projects to feature sculptural form, and it marked Frank Gehry as an "authentic original." This "rumpled, humorous and intense man," as he was known, was off to a good start. But as Gehry knew well, life could be happy and sad at the same time.

In 1968 he and Anita were divorced. He felt fortunate that he had his work to occupy him during the breakup of his family. His work at the time was not limited to designing buildings. Like his father, who had made a brief foray into the furniture business, Gehry applied his talent to a line of furniture—but one unlike any other. Between 1969 and 1973, he created pieces of furniture out of corrugated cardboard.

The furniture was strong enough to sit or lie on—like his father's papier-mâché horse. His creative furniture line, called Easy Edges, consisted of playful forms that were cheap and popular. Though the future looked bright, Gehry gave up the furniture business to focus on architecture.

Gehry designed this chair made of corrugated cardboard.

Gehry found a new focus in his personal life as well. In 1975 he married Berta Aguilera from Panama, and she became his office manager. After their two sons, Alejandro and Samuel, were born in 1976 and 1979, Frank and Berta realized that they had outgrown their crowded apartment. Yet Gehry couldn't afford to build the kind of house he wanted for his family. After a careful search, they bought a small pink house in Santa Monica, about thirteen miles south of Los Angeles. Because he was his own client, he was free to remodel it as he wished.

Gehry transformed his home in Santa Monica, California, into a creation of his own design.

Chapter FOUR

"I'M NOT WEIRD"

IN 1977 THE SPACE SHUTTLE *ENTERPRISE* MADE ITS first gliding test flight. But on a quiet street in Santa Monica, California, the most earth-shaking event that year was Frank Gehry's remodeled house.

To his neighbors, the house looked like something the *Enterprise* might have brought back from outer space. One woman was so shocked to see Gehry's house covered in steel and chain-link fencing that she tried to sue him. But critics praised the project. "[It is] a major work of architecture—perhaps the most significant new house in Southern California in some years," critic Paul Goldberger wrote in the *New York Times*.

And Philip Johnson, then considered the leader of U.S. architecture, said, "His buildings are shocking.

The Taj Mahal is a tomb that Indian ruler Shah Jahan had built for his wife in the 1600s. The tomb is located in northern India. It is an example of balanced, symmetrical architecture.

They don't please the eye the way the Taj Mahal [world-famous seventeenth-century tomb in India] does, but they give you a mysterious feeling of delight."

Before designing a house or any building, architects usually ask themselves how the building can be both useful and pleasing to look at. What shapes, colors, and textures will blend in with and improve the other buildings in the area? How will this building fit in with the natural environment surrounding the site?

Can the architect meet all the client's needs and still build a work of art?

Since Gehry was his own client, he didn't have to answer to anyone. At first, he was going to leave the outside of his house the way it was—faded pink and somewhat run-down—while he made radical changes inside. He started by stripping down the walls and ceilings to expose the beams and rafters underneath. But he couldn't resist doing something different to the outside too, as journalist Joseph Morgenstern described in the *New York Times Magazine*.

> He enclosed the whole house in a startling sheath [cover] of corrugated steel and rough, utility-grade plywood, with a chain-link extravaganza that suggests a Little League backstop and a kitchen window that looks like a giant ice cube trying to escape.

(Because he used inexpensive, human-made materials, Gehry referred to his house as "cheapskate architecture.")

GROWING UP IN A JUNGLE GYM

Frank and Berta's sons, Alejandro (Alejo), six, and Samuel, two and one-half, loved growing up in the remodeled house. For them it was like "living in a combination jungle gym and movie back lot." In some areas, Gehry used reflected light to create a mysterious feeling of being in outer space. He also used soft lighting to provide cozy, warm places for family and friends to talk and relax.

Like any true work of art, Gehry's house reflects the person who made it. Memories of his childhood, such as the dark stairway like the one in his grandparents' house, can be found inside. Parts of the house are neat and orderly and recall the influence of Frank's mother. Other spaces are jumbled—with surprising exits and entrances that recall the unsettled feeling created by Gehry's father.

But the outside of the house continued to shock people. Gehry reminded them that there were metal trucks, boats, and campers parked in front of their houses, so why should they be startled by the metal walls on the outside of his house? In fact, he painted part of a wall aqua as a playful way of blending with the neighbors' blue and green trucks.

Gehry insisted that he did not try to shock people with his house. But because of the controversy it caused, he was afraid it might scare away potential clients he needed for his company to succeed.

During the 1980s, Gehry designed structures in France, Germany, and Japan, but his best-known projects were built in his home state of California. The Loyola Marymount University administration asked Gehry to design a mini-campus for the law school in downtown Los Angeles. The administration wanted his design to enliven the life at the school. Gehry faced a big challenge. He met with Loyola personnel to talk about his vision of the project—how he imagined it to be. He also listened to the needs of the student body, faculty, and administration.

IT'S GREEK TO HIM

Gehry's vision of a law school campus was a group of buildings, like an Acropolis, with stairs leading up to it. The word *acropolis* is Greek for "elevated city." The

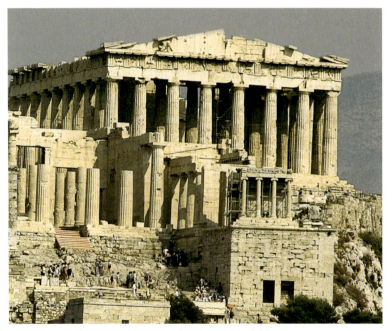

The ruins of the Parthenon, built in the fifth century B.C. as part of the Acropolis in Athens, Greece, are now a tourist attraction.

most famous acropolis was built in Athens, Greece, in the fifth century B.C. The Greeks developed ideas about proportion and harmony that still influence modern-day architects. Gehry also imagined the Roman Forum in Rome, Italy, where the foundation of civil law (the body of law that governs the rights of private individuals) was formed. And he thought of the law students and their needs. "A client hires me to make my dreams real, to grab that image and hold it, crystallize it into reality," he said. In 1981 he began to do just that.

That year the California Council of the American Institute of Architects named Gehry Architect of the Year. After the award ceremony, he gave a speech titled "I'm Not Weird." Gehry hoped to reassure the public that he was "a standard architect.... I do drawings like everyone else. I get building permits. I meet schedules and budgets," he said. As commissions, or jobs, came in, Gehry showed how architecture could bring people together and lift their spirits.

Before Gehry went to work on the Loyola campus, students had no area on the grounds to gather between classes, to talk, to exchange ideas, or to just relax. The older buildings on the campus created a depressing atmosphere for learning and studying, so Gehry tried a fresh look. He used a bright reddish rust stucco (a durable finish of cement, sand, and lime) on the outside of the student center, and plywood and glass on alternating sides of the school's chapel. He also created a courtyard to bring students together. He placed four concrete columns outside the moot court (a mock court where law students practice their courtroom techniques). The columns

Gehry incorporated aspects of the Acropolis into his design for the Loyola Law School in downtown Los Angeles.

are reminders of the columns of the Acropolis in Greece and the Roman Forum in Italy. But Gehry designed his columns on a more human scale—shorter, stubbier, more down-to-earth than those found in Athens or Rome.

He added two small classroom buildings and a larger, combined classroom and office building. He believes that clusters of small buildings create a more intimate, friendlier atmosphere than the glass-box type of modern architecture.

That belief can also be seen in the Cabrillo Marine Museum in San Pedro, California. The museum features

Gehry's design for the Cabrillo Marine Museum in San Pedro, California, incorporates chain link.

four small, white buildings connected by Gehry's creative use of chain link. To Philip Johnson, the chain link looked "awful." But Gehry pointed out that chain link reminded children of playgrounds, and most of the museum's visitors were children. Once inside the museum, children found many surprises, as described by Joseph Morgenstern:

> You can see the aquarium tanks in the conventional way, walking past them through darkened, worm-like tunnels, or you can take a backstage route to see what marine biologists really do. Back stage is more fun, of course, with the staff at their cluttered worktables in a nautical-industrial environment of unfinished ceilings, exposed ducts, and white pipes.... The museum is bright and inviting like a sun-drenched submarine.

WHY NOT CHAIN LINK?

The Cabrillo Marine Museum enchanted Los Angeles mayor Tom Bradley. He couldn't believe it could be built at such a low cost to the city. "You did all this for $3 million?" he asked the museum director in amazement.

As Gehry's commissions increased throughout Southern California, so did the budgets for some of his buildings. The $50 million shopping mall in Santa Monica, completed in the early 1980s, also featured a drape of chain link—about three hundred feet long and six stories high—on one exterior wall. It was covered with huge chain-link letters in a different color, spelling SANTA MONICA PLACE. Whenever he was asked why he used so much chain link, Gehry had a ready-made answer. Chain link is cheap, and it's all around us—"in quantities sufficient to fence in the moon"—so why not use it? He felt the same way about sunlight. It's there, so let's use it.

Gehry used chain link to spell out the name Santa Monica Place *along the side of the shopping-mall building.*

Gehry used light to bring the outdoors indoors throughout Santa Monica Place. After working all week in the mall, one employee drove fifty miles back to Santa Monica Place to shop on weekends. "I know it seems strange," she said, "but this place is so light and airy; most shopping malls are like jails."

While Gehry designed many structures from scratch, he also loved the challenge of transforming old buildings into something new and exciting. He seemed to be on a roll, and nothing was going to stop him.

Gehry designed an exhibition of Russian avant-garde art for the Los Angeles County Museum of Art.

Chapter **FIVE**

IMAGININGS

GEHRY'S LOVE OF ART—PAINTING AND SCULPTURE, in particular—can be seen in the designs he did for exhibitions at the Los Angeles County Museum of Art. Once a collection is assembled for exhibition, museum staffers deal with some basic questions. How should the works be displayed? What is the best way to attract the viewer to the art? How can the placement of walls or partitions and their color and texture affect the art? Where should the entrances and exits be placed for easy access?

Viewers and critics alike applauded Gehry's solutions to such problems. Art Treasures in Japan, The Treasures of Tutankhamen (Tutankhamen was king of Egypt from 1361–1352 B.C.), The Avant-Garde in Russia, and Seventeen Artists in the Sixties were among the exhibitions for which Gehry designed spaces in the Los Angeles County Museum of Art. Critics gave his exhibition designs high praise.

In 1982 Gehry transformed a dreary building—the old Los Angeles Armory—into the California Aerospace Museum. One look at the building tells that it is about aerospace because Gehry designed a jet fighter plane as part of the exterior wall.

The following year, the American Academy and Institute of Arts and Letters awarded the 1983 Arnold W. Brunner Prize to Gehry. The prize is given to "an architect who has made a significant contribution to architecture as art."

IMAGININGS

Long before Gehry builds a model of a proposed project, he notes his "fleeting images" on paper. He makes sketch models—or "imaginings"—that serve as important tools to spark original thinking.

Gehry refers to the initial drawings for all of his projects as a kind of frantic searching for solutions. The drawings have even become sought-after works of art exhibited in both Paris and New York.

In 1983 Gehry designed a guesthouse for the home of Penny and David Winton in Wayzata, Minnesota. The Wintons chose Gehry after meeting with him, looking at his work, and listening carefully to his ideas. "It was Frank's confidence—his sure hand—

EDUCATION GEHRY STYLE

Gehry's sketch models and the other techniques that he uses to stir the imagination had a profound influence on his younger sister, Doreen Nelson. She pioneered a theory of education, known as Design Based Learning. "My close-hand look at Frank's work has been helpful in my own," she said. And it is not surprising that Frank was one of the first to serve on Doreen's board of advisory trustees.

Gehry's interest in children's natural creativity can be seen in his buildings. In addition to the Cabrillo Marine Museum, he designed the Arts Park in San Fernando Valley and the Los Angeles Children's Museum. All three museums are designed to invite children to learn by doing. He also helped the Los Angeles school system, the National Endowment for the Arts, and the Smithsonian Institution develop programs to interest young people in city planning. Studying the problems of city planning can be fun for children, Gehry says, if they are given the freedom to imagine and the time to create their own models. "It has been demonstrated that this subject [city planning] is intensely interesting to both children and the teens," wrote famed architect-inventor Buckminster Fuller, and "one of the most important... subjects of *real* education."

that impressed us so," Penny Winton said. "And his desire to reflect our personal interests in the architecture... to make it a place that children would love... inspired the design and pleased us immensely."

The Winton Guesthouse in Wayzata, Minnesota, is an early example of Gehry's use of sculpted forms in his architecture.

The Winton Guesthouse won praise from architectural critics. The guesthouse was, in fact, a group of small one-room buildings, which, viewed together, appear to be sculptured forms. Gehry once wrote:

> I approach each building as a sculptural object, a spatial container, a space with light and air.... To this container, this sculpture, the user brings his baggage, his program, and interacts with it to accommodate his needs. If I can't do that, I've failed.

A photograph of Constantin Brancusi, the famous Romanian sculptor, that sits on Gehry's desk reminds visitors of the influence of sculpture on Gehry's work. "[Brancusi] has had more influence on my work than most architects," he said. It is easy to see why. Brancusi's works are known for their simplicity. His extraordinary ability to transform natural objects to their simplest forms has placed him among the most influential artists in the history of modern art. Gehry no doubt recalled the carp in the bathtub from his childhood when he first saw Brancusi's *Golden Fish*.

Gehry's friendships with artists, including Coosje Van Bruggen, Peter Alexander, Chuck Arnoldi, Ed Moses, Billy Al Bengstron, Ed Ruscha, and Claes Oldenburg, also have influenced his work and illuminated his life. In fact, his friendships with these artists early in his career really changed everything for Gehry. At that time, other architects disregarded him. The artistic community in Venice, California, during the 1970s embraced him. He even worked with Oldenburg and his wife, Coosje Van Bruggen, on the Chiat/Day Office in Venice, California. Oldenburg and Van

Constantin Brancusi

Constantin Brancusi, a Romanian sculptor who worked in France in the early twentieth century, became famous for his use of streamlined, geometric forms. Brass, marble, wood, and stone were his favorite materials. Instead of sculpting every detail of a subject's face or an object's parts, Brancusi dared to turn the figure into one sweeping, smooth form that aroused the viewer's imagination. A sleek, shiny shape rising from its base would make one think of a bird in space. A rounded form lying at a slant on its base would remind one of a person at rest.

Brancusi's ultrasimplified *Bird in Space* set off a firestorm of controversy in the 1920s. It has become one of the most influential works of modern art. He was influenced by African sculpture, which was well known for its simplicity and solid forms.

Bird in Space

Art that does not represent an object in its exact form, or greatly simplifies it, is called abstract art. Brancusi was an early explorer of abstract sculpture. Though one can find something real in his sculpture, such as the rounded shape of a person's head or shapes that suggest parts of the body, it is the whole form that viewers remember, wonder about, and discuss. Some called his work primitive. Some called it mysterious. Others didn't know what to call it.

One thing was certain: it was new.

It is easy to see Brancusi's influence on Frank Gehry, who loves to work with highly polished materials and to explore new ways to use them. And like Brancusi's sculpture, Gehry's buildings continue to bewitch and bewilder viewers around the world.

Bruggen created a pair of forty-five-foot binoculars for the building's entrance. An office and library are housed in the shafts of the binoculars.

Gehry's humorous touches and use of ordinary materials caused some viewers to question his seriousness. But Paul Goldberger of the *New York Times* reminded viewers that Gehry's work "is vastly more intelligent and controlled than it sounds" to those unfamiliar with bold new architectural design. "[Gehry] is an architect of immense gifts" who keeps art and architecture in perfect harmony. He achieves an exact balance between the two art forms."

Frank Gehry, Claes Oldenburg, and Coosje Van Bruggen designed the Chiat/Day Office in Venice, California.

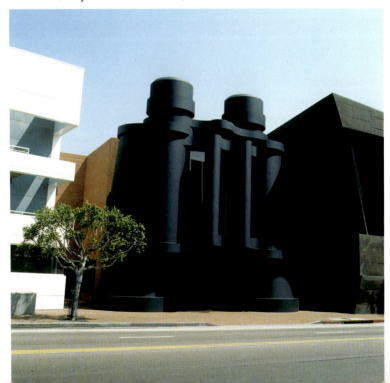

Gone Fishing

During the 1980s, Gehry's projects multiplied. The Formica Corporation chose him to create designs using its plastic laminate Colorcore. (Laminate is made of various materials compressed into thin plates or sheets.) Gehry was unhappy with his first designs and decided to break a sample of the material to examine it more closely. Right away, he noticed that the broken pieces looked like fish scales. The result? He made laminated lamps in the form of fish, and snakelike lamps followed shortly afterward.

In 1986 the fish and snake lamps were included in a major exhibition of Gehry's work at the Walker Art Center in Minneapolis, Minnesota. From there, the exhibit traveled to other major cities, including Atlanta, Georgia; Houston, Texas; Toronto, Ontario, in Canada; Los Angeles, California; and New York, New York.

The exhibition included everything from Gehry's sketches to his cardboard furniture. Five room-size structures displayed models of spaces he had designed. A huge fish-shaped enclosure (made of copper and lead scales) that contained the fish and snake lamps was a major attraction. But Gehry's twenty-two-foot-tall fish sculpture was the piece that most delighted viewers. The response prompted the Walker to purchase the fish sculpture, which was made of squares of glass that resembled scales, for the museum's permanent collection.

Imaginings 47

Gehry designed his sculpture, Fish, *for the 1992 Olympics.*

In 1989 Gehry began a monumental fish sculpture for the Olympic Village for the 1992 Olympics in Barcelona, Spain. Ever since his childhood and those special Thursdays at his grandparents' house, the movement of the fish had remained a vivid image in his mind. Gehry had an intense interest in movement—studying it and trying to incorporate a sense of movement into static, or immobile, materials.

The Olympics fish sculpture marked a turning point in the history of Frank O. Gehry & Associates. For the first time, the firm used a computer-aided design and manufacturing program in its work. The firm adopted computer aided three-dimensional interactive application (CATIA). Without this, some of Gehry's most exciting buildings could not have been possible. Although Gehry designs using sketches and physical models, the computer can check those designs before construction. The computer simplifies the construction process.

Gehry is pictured here in 1982 in Santa Monica, California.

Meanwhile, Gehry was also teaching his ideas to a new generation of architects. Between 1980 and 1989, he taught at Harvard University's Graduate School of Design, Yale University, and the University of Southern California. He received honorary doctoral degrees from those institutions and many other universities throughout the world. The title that seems to fit him best, according to students, is that of teacher. As one Yale student recalled: Gehry is a "man who wanted to free people up rather than sell his own doctrines."

SPECIAL PRIZE

The Pritzker Architecture Prize is the most important architectural award in the United States. Chicago businessman Jay Pritzker and his wife Cindy founded the award, which honors excellence in architecture.

In 1989 Gehry was awarded the Pritzker Prize. At the award ceremony in Japan, the Pritzker committee stated, "In an artistic climate that too often looks backward rather than toward the future [and where following older designs is often safer than risking new ones], it is important to honor the architecture of Frank O. Gehry."

The Pritzker spokesperson praised Gehry for taking risks and designing buildings that show his "restless spirit." He praised the moving shapes and forms used in Gehry's work as reflecting the restless feeling shared by many people. "Although the prize is for a lifetime of achievement," the spokesperson said, he hoped that it would encourage Gehry to continue his "extraordinary work in progress." In his acceptance speech, Gehry said:

> Colleagues and friends... I love being here in Japan.... Today is a special honor for me, to receive this important prize. I am obsessed with architecture. It is true, I am restless, trying to find myself as an architect.... Architects must solve complex problems. We must understand and use technology, we must create buildings which are safe and dry, respectful of context and neighbors.... But then what? The moment of truth, the compositions of elements, the selection of forms, scale, materials, color, finally, all the same issues facing the painter and the sculptor. Architecture is surely an art....

Gehry went on to say that architects must solve difficult problems and please clients at the same time. City planning is difficult today, he said. "The dream is that each brick, each window, each road, each tree will be placed lovingly by craftsmen, client, architect, and people to create beautiful cities."

He spoke about the need to do better in the selection of materials and colors in the same way painters do. He insisted that architecture is a creative process that involves the same challenges that face all artists.

And he reminded listeners of the importance of technology and its many uses in architecture.

Gehry had already proved his firm's mastery in the field of modern technology in designing his large fish sculpture for the Olympics, and he knew there was more to discover about computer-aided design. In 1989 computers were becoming a common part of classrooms around the world. The need to explore and to learn never ends, according to Gehry. The challenge is to do better, he told the Pritzker Prize committee, "and finally bring greater honor to the prize, and that is what I intend to do." The award became the springboard for some of Gehry's most sensational and controversial work.

The Weisman Art Museum is located along the Mississippi River near downtown Minneapolis, Minnesota.

Chapter **SIX**

THE ART OF ARCHITECTURE

IN 1991 GEHRY'S DESIGN FOR THE FREDERICK R. Weisman Art Museum began to materialize on the banks of the Mississippi River in Minneapolis, Minnesota. Seeing it, many people asked, what is that? As it neared completion, still more questions arose about the University of Minnesota's newest building. It horrified some and delighted others. "A UFO has crashed on the campus!" one student said. It looks like "an exploding silver artichoke," another commented. At first glance, the cluster of stainless steel geometric forms on the building's exterior seemed to be on a collision course. "Isn't it exciting?" a passerby remarked. "It jazzes up the whole area.... I love it!"

After the initial shock wore off, Gehry's Weisman Art Museum became a landmark in Minneapolis and won high praise. The stainless steel forms seen from the west seem to be at odds with the older buildings on campus. But the rich rust color on the rectangular, concrete portion of the museum and the brick used on another part blends in with neighboring buildings on campus.

Gehry hoped that the Weisman's shiny, western exterior would stir the imaginations and curiosity of

Gehry (right) *stands with University of Minnesota president Robert H. Bruininks and Weisman director Lyndel King in 2003 at the tenth anniversary of the opening of the Weisman Art Museum.*

students and passersby. He hoped the museum would draw people to the campus and entice them to look at the art inside. "From the beginning it was clear that the client's interests come first to Frank Gehry," Weisman director Lyndel King said. "Early in the design process he listened carefully to our questions, our ideas, our goals—and our budget—and took them all very seriously."

The galleries inside are "a far cry from the anonymous boxes typical of museum architecture," according to author Kara Vander Weg. Natural light floods the interior. The ceiling features curving "slices" cut out of it to allow the outside light in. Like the exterior, the interior spaces become works of art themselves. Those who say that some of the art at the Weisman is "off the wall" are right!

New Explorations

Reflections from the river below cast a brilliant glow over the stainless steel western exterior. At sunset the shiny panels reflect brilliant oranges and yellows and win the competition with the setting sun. The metallic sheen, or luster, changes color according to the time of day and the position of the sun. It is architecture "in perpetual motion," like Gehry himself.

The Weisman Museum seemed to fulfill some of Gehry's ideas for a house he had designed for businessman Peter Lewis in Cleveland, Ohio, but was never built. The design was a good example of Gehry's creative use of computer software. The design became a laboratory for experimentation. The computer served as a tool for developing Gehry's visions—not for making actual forms. It gave him more freedom to design than ever before.

The Big Show

The city of Bilbao had been in deep financial trouble during the 1980s. Though it was the largest city in northern Spain, it was on the verge of becoming a slum. Shipyards and steel plants had shut down due to rising competition from other areas. The unemployment rate soared, making life almost unbearable in Bilbao.

Could the city ever regain its past reputation as one of Spain's richest industrial centers? What could the city do to restore its glorious past? Was it even possible to do so? Those were some of the basic questions that faced the city leaders.

They answered those questions by building a new railway station, a shopping center, a new airport, and other necessary features that help make a city work. Yet the town needed something dramatic to put it in the spotlight, to attract visitors and businesses alike. Government leaders turned to the Solomon R. Guggenheim Foundation. It operates the legendary Guggenheim Museum in New York City. The foundation also operates an empire of art collections around the world. Thomas Krens, head of the Guggenheim Museum in New York, invited three architects—from

The Art of Architecture

Models are an important part of the design process for architects. This is a model of the Art Gallery of Ontario, a project designed by Gehry Partners in 2004.

Austria, Japan, and the United States—to submit plans. Gehry presented a remarkable plan for a site along the Nervión River, which runs through Bilbao. He created his model out of wood, foam core, and paper. Gehry's plan clearly surpassed the other two. But could it actually be built?

FROM GRAY TO GOLD TO RED

Soon after Gehry had been selected as the architect of the new museum, local Bilbao residents began to ask, *Quien es Frank Gehry?* (Who is Frank Gehry?) They soon found out. In 1991 Gehry and his team geared

The CATIA Advantage

Frank Gehry's large fish sculpture designed for the 1992 Olympics was his first computer-aided design. Financial and scheduling restrictions prompted James Glymph, a partner in Gehry's firm, to look for a computer program that would make construction easier and faster. The search led to CATIA, computer aided three-dimensional interactive application. The program was first developed by the French aerospace industry.

CATIA is a three-dimensional modeling program. Gehry can make a physical model of a particular design. A penlike device on the computer traces the shape of the physical model. This transfers the shape to the computer. It can then produce an accurate electronic model. After the computer model is created, it becomes the basis of a fully detailed model. That model is used to guide the assembly of materials and construction.

The program can aid in design, manufacturing, and engineering. It can test design structure and get accurate cost estimates by providing exact dimensions to other people involved in building the actual structure. As a result, Gehry's firm uses CATIA to develop complex designs within set boundaries.

up for the Bilbao project and the awesome task of injecting new life into a disintegrating city.

Gehry had used the computer software program CATIA on earlier projects, but he used it to the fullest in constructing the new Guggenheim

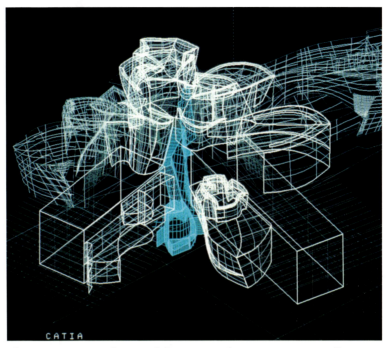

This computer rendering of the Guggenheim Museum in Bilbao was created using the CATIA program.

Museum in Bilbao. CATIA did not serve as a tool in the design process, but it checked the design and helped to keep costs down. It also made construction plans easier.

Gehry used titanium (a silvery gray metallic element) on the exterior of the Guggenheim Museum. "Thin titanium planes project from the ground and float like strange jellyfish against the sky," architecture critic Steen Estvad Petersen wrote. Located on the Nervión River, the building reflects the river's wavy motion, and depending on the sun and time of day, the titanium changes from gray to gold to red—much like the Weisman Museum on the Mississippi River.

The sweeping forms and reflective materials used in both the Guggenheim in Bilbao (above) *and the Weisman in Minneapolis have become trademarks of Gehry's buildings.*

Like Gehry's early family life, marked by boom and bust, chaos and order, his design for the Guggenheim in Bilbao is full of contrasts. Rectangular spaces lead into circular galleries with curving walls. The galleries differ in design according to the art on exhibit. That is the art of architecture. And Gehry proved to be a master of it.

In his essay "Jumbo Architecture," in *Frank O. Gehry: The Architect's Studio*, Steen Petersen summarized the general impact of Gehry's Guggenheim Museum:

> The enormous atrium [skylighted court] towers up through the building like a Gothic cathedral and is spanned by concrete, steel, titanium, elevator shafts, walkways, and skylights in wild confusion.... Gehry's museum is a total rhythmic composition... which, depending on temperament [mood] and taste, can be experienced as a miracle or a nightmare.... Frank O. Gehry is a decided loner and perhaps the only living architect who has been fully able to eliminate the boundaries between art and architecture.

The Guggenheim in Bilbao not only restored the city's reputation but announced it around the world. And the incredible economic and cultural boom that resulted became known as "the Bilbao effect." No one in Bilbao asks, *Quien es Frank Gehry?* anymore!

Gehry designed the Experience Music Project in downtown Seattle, Washington. The Space Needle is seen in the background.

Chapter **SEVEN**

"SWOOPY" IN SEATTLE

FRANK GEHRY DOESN'T WASTE TIME SEEKING THE limelight or basking in the glory of success. Always in motion, he is never without projects to work on. But in 1994, his mother's death seemed to give him a different view of the importance of everything else. She had been a beacon for both Frank and his sister, Doreen. She had been "the intellectual force in our lives," Doreen said. Thelma had taken her children to art galleries and concerts, and she encouraged their creative activities and ideas. "By valuing our own ideas she helped to build our self-esteem," Doreen said. Both Frank and Doreen focused on their work—just as their mother had done during sad and tough times.

In 1997 Gehry was awarded the Friedrich Kiesler Prize, sponsored by the Republic of Austria, the city of Vienna, and private sponsors, for "the courage and the... freedom with which he creates his buildings." The prize, in honor of architect and designer Friedrich Kiesler, is awarded every other year for extraordinary achievement in architecture and related arts.

During the 1990s, Gehry was thrilled to be able to combine his love of music with his architecture. Two major projects absorbed his time and talent (or as Gehry says, "this funny talent I've got"). The first celebrated popular music, and the second, classical music.

Before Gehry designed the Experience Music Project in Seattle, Washington, he asked his client, Microsoft cofounder Paul Allen, what he had in mind for the structure. Allen, a fan of rock-and-roll guitar player Jimi Hendrix, said he wanted something "swoopy." "Swoopy" was music to Gehry's ears! He would try to make his building appear to roll—giving a clue to the rock-and-roll music to be heard inside. It was the kind of challenge Gehry loved.

Though the initial challenge of any project "makes him nervous," modeling it in miniature with his associates both calms his nerves and excites him. Journalist and screenwriter Joseph Morgenstern described a design meeting that took place at a table in Gehry's office:

Gehry and his associates were not sure they had found the final form.... They juggled the [balsa wood and cardboard] elements. Gehry, who did most of the juggling, moved a little cardboard tube an inch. "You like this?" Gehry asked. An associate shrugged. Silence for a while. "Or maybe like so. It'd be nice putting these little guys on a pedestal." Another associate shrugged.... "What about tearing these corners out? Let's see what we get." Gehry did the deed with his X-Acto (knife). More silence. More contemplation. "Well? What do you think?" "I like it better the other way," the first young man finally said. "It's more dreamlike." Gehry nodded gravely. Then he grinned.

Gehry's respect for team play is at the heart of his success. Currently, his architectural firm employs more than 135 people. Until his son Sam, a young architect, returned to school to study art, he too worked at the firm. His son, Alejandro, an artist, has also worked on some projects for the firm.

Frank's daughters seem to have inherited their father's artistic talent too. Brina works for the Sesame Workshop, and Leslie is a graphic designer. Yet Gehry becomes so absorbed in his work that he tends to forget personal things and regrets doing so. "I love my kids, my wife, but I'm so intensely involved.... I never remember anything personal," he has said. But he never misses a chance to play hockey with Sam and

Weisman director Lyndel King referees hockey practice between Gehry's office team (Gehry wears number 13) and supporters of the Weisman Museum in 1993.

Alejandro. At the age of sixty-eight, Gehry learned the sport so he could share it with his sons. "You know the greatest thing in life is to have your kids ask you to play with them," he said. He even organized a hockey team at the office.

ON THE MOVE

Gehry likes to bring people of all ages together, and the Experience Music Project, the rock-and-roll center in Seattle, does that. The project features Gehry's lively forms and colors. The curving metal exterior creates the rolling effect Gehry wanted. And the glass sculpture across the top reminds music fans of the

"Swoopy" in Seattle 67

strings and frets (ridges under the strings) on the neck of a guitar. The idea for the sculpture came from experiments with broken pieces of a guitar. An existing monorail, a small train on a single track, runs through the building to the Seattle Center—a convention and entertainment center near downtown Seattle. Instead of being a distraction, the rolling movement of the monorail tends to blend right in with the rock-and-roll theme.

The variety of colors covering the glass sculpture also links the outside to the inside. Red, silver, gold, blue, and purple remind viewers of rock-and-roll songs—particularly "Purple Haze" by Jimi Hendrix.

On a Quieter Note

In 1995 Gehry's friend Maggie Jencks died of breast cancer. In 1999 a foundation created before her death, Maggie's Centre, asked Gehry to design one of several centers that it ran. In her honor, Gehry waived his fee for the project. Maggie's Centre, located in Dundee, Scotland, opened in 2003 and was Gehry's first building in the United Kingdom. In 2004 the center won the Royal Fine Art Commission's British Building of the Year award.

Construction on the Walt Disney Concert Hall began in 1987. By 2002 it was near completion.

Chapter **EIGHT**

MIRACLE ON FIRST STREET

THE EXPERIENCE MUSIC PROJECT SEEMED TO STRIKE the first chord of an even bigger musical experience in Los Angeles. After a delay due to funding problems, the Walt Disney Concert Hall finally moved toward its 2003 completion date. A lover of contrasts, Gehry could balance a rock-and-roll museum and a concert hall with the greatest of ease.

For a while, the Walt Disney Concert Hall seemed doomed. Construction came to a halt under the pressure of rising costs and disputes between city officials and orchestra patrons. Lillian Disney, Walt Disney's widow, had donated $50 million to build the hall. But it was not enough. When she died in 1997, her daughter, Diane Disney Miller, stepped in on her mother's behalf and secured the funds necessary to finish the project. Finally, in 2003, after sixteen years of off-and-on construction at a cost of $274 million, the concert hall was completed. "It got built," Gehry said, "and that's a miracle."

To many who visit the hall, the building itself is a miracle—a miracle on the corner of Grand Avenue and First Street in downtown Los Angeles. The site was familiar to Gehry, because it was just two miles away from the small apartment where he had lived with his parents and sister after their arrival from Canada. The location gave the concert hall a personal connection unlike any other major building he had designed.

When Gehry won the design competition for the Disney Concert Hall, he was especially thrilled. He had always wanted to design a major building in the city where he had lived most of his life. Although he had designed other structures in and around Los Angeles, none could compare to the Disney Concert Hall in scope.

Lillian Disney, however, was not thrilled at the selection of Gehry as designer—at first. A lover of gardens and everything floral, her vision of the concert hall was far removed from Gehry's, but she did not say so directly. Gehry did receive a photo from her showing a "thatched hut and a little pond with duckies ... and weeping willows," which she liked. But Gehry said that "if we did that, it would soon be called Disneyland instead of a concert hall."

Miracle on First Street   71

Lillian Disney made no demands regarding Gehry's design, and she never tried to veto any of his ideas. "We promised Los Angeles a Frank Gehry building, and that's what we intend to deliver," Diane Disney Miller told the *New York Times*.

OVERCOMING OBSTACLES

Gehry 's curving metal forms began to sail around the building, as construction resumed. Although the steel forms differ from his previous buildings in proportion

Gehry's quick sketch captures the overall feeling and design of the Walt Disney Concert Hall. Gehry's drawings are sought after by museums and art collectors around the world.

and shape, still, they shimmer, they soar, and they form a landmark in Los Angeles. "I like to walk around and look at it from the streets, seeing it like a flower between the [other] buildings," Gehry said as he toured the building before its official opening. "You don't see the whole of it, you see flecks of it." He points out the steps that were designed "for people to sit on with their lunches, with brown bags," and the public garden, which is open during the day for everyone to enjoy.

Gehry, who is a weekend sailor, likes to talk about the building in nautical terms, as if it were a ship. He describes the interior of the concert hall as a "magical barge," gift wrapped in silver. "It's a fantastic cocoon of honey-colored Douglas fir, with a ceiling of billowing wood, partly open across its 'stern' so daylight seeps in," journalist Cathleen McGuigan reported in *Newsweek* magazine. The seats in the hall are covered with a floral pattern, and the floral motif is repeated in the carpet. "I promised Mrs. Disney," Gehry said, remembering his promise to honor her love of gardens.

Also in honor of Lillian Disney, artist Thomas Osinski created the Lillian Disney Memorial Fountain—a huge rose made of broken pieces of delft china, which she collected. (Delft is a creamy white pottery with designs painted on it, often in blue. It is named for the town of Delft in the Netherlands.) The public garden adjacent to the building honors her as well. More than fifty trees and numerous plants grow there.

Gehry made his mark on Los Angeles with the design of the Walt Disney Concert Hall.

The concert hall complex includes a children's amphitheater, which seats three hundred people. "It's all about community," says Gehry. "Children will hear performances, [like] 'Peter and the Wolf,' and they'll start to come in. In Germany, young kids line up for unclaimed tickets, and that doesn't happen here. I think it's because of the failure of our musical education. We have a lot to overcome."

But it is the interior of the main hall—the auditorium—that amazes audiences. The sound is exceptional from all seats throughout the auditorium. (Music is not for the upper class only, Gehry insists.)

The interior space of the Walt Disney Concert Hall was designed to enhance the sound of the live music that is played there.

LOVE AT FIRST SIGHT?

s the Walt Disney Concert Hall neared completion on the corner of First Street and Grand Avenue in Los Angeles, the public didn't hesitate to speak out about Frank Gehry's new building. Young and old alike greeted the new landmark with a wide range of responses:

"The building is just ridiculous. I love it," said Harout Senekeremian, a twenty-year-old senior at Oberlin Conservatory of Music, Oberlin, Ohio.

"It's all stainless steel. No windows. . . . It's as if someone hung pans out there," Marie Bustillos, a nearby city employee said.

I've just gotten more and more excited as it's gone up," said Nicholas Pappone, a fifteen-year-old violinist. "I think it's one of the best things to happen to classical music here."

"It's so big it should be in Texas," Eva A. Plasencio, a seventy-eight-year-old Texas resident said.

"You are awestruck by it the first time you see it up close. You think, that's insane. Good insane. . . . Now we have the coolest concert hall in the country," fifteen-year-old bassist Noah Reitman said.

Peter Elliot, a seventy-year-old neighbor, said, "It's definitely not a box."

"It's spectacular—and I've been in a lot of halls," cellist Yo-Yo Ma said.

"Everyone wants to touch it," said one of the maintenance crew while rubbing handprints off the stainless steel exterior.

One thing is certain: Gehry's buildings bring people together and inspire lively talk, and nothing pleases the architect more than that.

The auditorium is more like a rounded space than a "room." Its wood walls move "up and in like giant clam shells."

Gehry likes to be alone in his "steel flower" and to look at the famous pipe organ that seems to explode from the wall. It has been described in many ways—from a forest of winter trees bursting from the wall to a bunch of french fries to a stack of lumber that has just exploded. The hall's exterior invites a variety of comments ranging from a "sparkling steel artichoke" to "a dead aluminum bird."

But professional critics rave. "Absolutely breathtaking," says Julius Shulman, the eminent Southern California architectural photographer. "It simply stands out as the best thing in Los Angeles," says longtime historian Robert Winter. And Christopher Knight, a *Los Angeles Times* critic, wrote, "Above the front entrance to Disney Hall great sheets of glistening stainless steel seem to peel away from each other like thin sheets of paper being torn in two. The design allows daylight to tumble into the building through glazed windows. But it also [gives] a feeling of [wonderful] escape, as if a powerful invisible force is bursting forth from inside the concert hall and out into the city."

That force would be music—music by the Los Angeles Philharmonic Orchestra. But the most important element of any concert hall is the acoustic (sound) system. If the sound system doesn't work well, all the dazzling features of the architecture mean little. "This stunning building will truly succeed only if the quality of its sound matches its physical beauty," Cathleen McGuigan reported in *Newsweek*. To ensure that perfect match, Gehry worked with Yasuhisa Toyota, a renowned specialist in sound systems.

OPENING NIGHT

On opening night, October 23, 2003, cameras flashed as movie stars joined government officials and music lovers from all over the world for the debut of the Walt Disney Concert Hall. More than 2,250 people arrived for the glittering event. Hundreds of reporters were ready with their microphones to catch visitors' responses to Gehry's new masterpiece. Concertgoers marveled at the building's exterior. It seemed to light up all of downtown Los Angeles. Some complained that rows of seats in the hall's interior were too close together and difficult to move around in, but rave reviews continued.

The opening night concert ended with Russian composer Igor Stravinsky's *Rite of Spring*, whose new sounds and rhythms shocked people when it was first played in 1913. According to Los Angeles musicologist Jean Shaw, the music was most appropriate for the debut of Gehry's new concert hall. When the piece ended, Esa Pekka Salonen, the music director, asked Gehry and Yasuhisa Toyota to join him on stage. And after an eight-minute standing ovation, silver confetti

Los Angeles Philharmonic music director Esa Pekka Salonen (left), *Yasuhisa Toyota* (middle), *and Gehry* (right) *received a standing ovation at the opening of the Walt Disney Concert Hall.*

sprayed down from the ceiling—like millions of tiny stars. "I think of it as a miracle," Gehry said. "I'm so far from the original thinking of it that I'm detached. So I look at it and I can't believe it's here, and I think, 'I must have thought of all these details but I don't remember when....'"

As neighborhood artist Louise Fletcher said of the concert hall: "I liked it from the beginning... its sprouting and it's telling you this music is for everybody." And from the beginning, that was what Frank Gehry aimed to prove through his architecture.

This model shows Gehry's design for one of the galleries of the Ohr-O'Keefe Museums in Biloxi, Mississippi.

Chapter **NINE**

THE BILOXI EFFECT?

IN 2003 GEHRY HEARD ABOUT A PROPOSAL FOR the new Ohr-O'Keefe Museums, named after potter George Ohr and Jeremiah O'Keefe, a financial supporter. Gehry jumped at the chance to design the new museums in Biloxi, Mississippi. He had seen a collection of Ohr's pottery at a friend's house. "It knocked my socks off," he recalled.

The directors of the Ohr-O'Keefe Museums were thrilled to have a world-famous architect design their building. Biloxi city leaders were impressed too and helped the museum directors find an attractive site for the new building, overlooking the Gulf of Mexico. When Gehry visited the site, he was elated. Clusters of oak trees adorned with Spanish moss provided a beautiful natural setting, which he was determined to preserve. "If the museum had been one large building," he said, the city "would have had to tear down some of the oaks. But once I saw those trees, I created pavilions to dance with them."

DESIGNING IN HARMONY

Though the museum was small, it presented a big challenge for Gehry. He did not want his architecture to distract from the beautiful pottery on exhibit. He was concerned that comparisons might be made between Gehry's curving forms and Ohr's free-flowing pottery. "Anything I designed that looked like what I'd been doing would have seemed like a spoof of Ohr," he said.

To avoid that problem, Gehry created three pavilions with walls that gently curve outward to enhance Ohr's rounded, flowing pottery—an estimated three hundred pieces, including one donated by Gehry. The museum, scheduled to open in July 2006, will also include a gallery to honor African American folk art, a ceramics studio, a library, and a gazebo (a small, open-sided structure) on the roof where visitors can enjoy the view of the surrounding trees and the Gulf.

"We were about to lose our heritage unless we let people know there was a lot more to Biloxi than casinos," Jermiah O'Keefe said. Can Gehry do for Biloxi what he did for Bilbao? Local residents are already

The Biloxi Effect? 83

Ohr's rounded, flowing pottery will be displayed at the Ohr-O'Keefe Museums.

looking forward to "the Biloxi effect." Nothing would please Gehry more than to design a museum that would attract an international audience to the work of George Ohr. And nothing would have amazed the Biloxi potter more than that.

WHO WAS GEORGE OHR?

eorge Ohr died in 1918, long before his work was recognized. The accidental way in which it was discovered intrigues creative people such as Frank Gehry. Fifty years after Ohr's death, in 1968, James Carpenter, an antiques dealer who was touring the Gulf Coast area with his wife, made the discovery. He was looking for old car parts and stopped at Ohr Boys' Auto Repair in Biloxi, Mississippi, hoping to find some. While there, Ohr's son, Ojo Ohr, a man in his sixties, casually asked in his native Mississippi drawl, "Would y'all like to see some of my daddy's pottery?"

Carpenter wasn't interested, but his wife was curious. Ojo led the couple to the garage, where seven thousand pieces of pottery had been stored in crates since George Ohr's death. Some pieces were placed on tables. As reported in the *Smithsonian* magazine, "Ojo opened the doors to reveal the most amazing collection of pottery in the history of American ceramics."

At the time, few people outside of Biloxi—including Carpenter—had ever heard of George Ohr. But after that chance discovery, Ohr became known as one of the most original potters in the United States. Finally, he will have a museum designed by one of the most original architects in the United States.

A Slam Dunk for Gehry

Going from a small museum in Biloxi, Mississippi, to a gigantic basketball arena in Brooklyn, New York, posed no problem for Frank Gehry—even at the age of seventy-four.

On December 10, 2003, Gehry and business leader Bruce C. Ratner presented their master plan for an eight-hundred-thousand-square-foot arena, seating twenty thousand people, for the New Jersey Nets basketball team, a member of the National Basketball Association (NBA). Ratner expects the arena to be built in Brooklyn. The NBA began on Brooklyn playgrounds. Basketball stars such as Michael Jordan and Red Auerbach began their rise to fame there.

At that December conference, all-star Bernard King, Brooklyn borough president Marty Markowitz, and New York mayor Michael Bloomberg praised Gehry's plan for a multiuse complex called the Brooklyn Atlantic Yards. In addition to the basketball arena, the complex will include housing units, retail stores, and six acres of open public space that feature an arena rooftop garden and a running track that can become a skating rink in winter. "Gehry's unique urban design fits into the streetscape [layout of city streets] and provided new landmarks and public spaces to make this borough and our entire city proud," Mayor Bloomberg said.

"This is an important opportunity for everyone," Gehry said. And Bruce Ratner concluded that "the

Gehry (left) and New York mayor Rudolph Giuliani stand in front of Gehry's proposed model for a new Guggenheim Museum in New York City in 2000. The project was never completed due to funding and environmental problems.

Nets will be a huge draw for sports fans from throughout the borough and all of the New York metropolitan area, and we intend to give them a first-class team to root for—in a Frank Gehry arena as dynamic and remarkable as the borough it's named after."

The project, costing more than one billion dollars, will be the biggest one designed by Gehry's firm to date. The firm, originally named Frank O. Gehry & Associates, is now Gehry Partners. Gehry Partners operates several divisions, or companies, including Gehry Design and Gehry Technologies. Gehry Design

The Biloxi Effect? 87

works mainly on product design. Products include wristwatches, furniture, door and window handles and hardware, and a trophy for the World Cup of Hockey. Gehry Technologies was formed to create computer software programs and to educate the industry in its use.

This lamp was created by Gehry Design.

Gehry Partners has expanded into a large company employing more than one hundred people.

ALL HANDS ON DECK!

Gehry has come a long way—from the use of ordinary, inexpensive chain link to sleek, expensive titanium. Yet the passion behind his projects remains the same, regardless of the materials he uses or the size of his buildings. With the help of his wife, Berta, he runs his companies like a "tight ship"—a firmly controlled vessel with a strong captain at the helm. "What interests me," Gehry says, "is that you can be a control freak and still deliver the passion." He is like a teacher who demands hard work from students and inspires them at the same time.

What surprises people is that Gehry can be an international star and still be unmoved by his fast-growing fame. He is still the friendly, casual, rumpled person he was before he became a celebrity. Of course, fame was never his goal. Imagining new and better ways to design things—from wristwatches to art museums—was always his aim. "But like his seemingly free-form . . . buildings, Gehry harbors a fierce discipline and perfectionism beneath his casual demeanor," Cathleen McGuigan writes.

As he approached his seventy-fifth birthday, Gehry showed no signs of retiring. In fact, he was as enthusiastic as ever about a special new project in Toronto, Canada, in the very neighborhood where he grew up. It would mean going home—to the streets and parks where he played as a boy. "For a lot of years I thought Toronto had forgotten me," he said.

Gehry returned to Toronto, Canada, in 2004 to present his plans for the expansion of the Art Gallery of Ontario (AGO).

Chapter **TEN**

BACK TO THE FUTURE

GEHRY WAS EIGHTEEN YEARS OLD WHEN HE MOVED with his family from Canada to the United States. When he was chosen to transform the Art Gallery of Ontario in Toronto more than fifty-six years later, he was thrilled. Going back there was a personal journey unlike any other.

In February 2004, local residents couldn't wait to see Gehry's plans to revitalize their favorite museum. "The Art Gallery of Ontario is where I first experienced art as a child and it was Grange Park where I played, so this project means a great deal to me," Gehry told the *Toronto Star*. "The building we envision will connect the city and its people to great art and art experiences."

Before he unveiled his plans for the $190 million Transformation AGO, he recalled his early days in Toronto. "My grandparents lived on Beverly Street just north of Queen, right near the AGO. I know the neighborhood, and I know the streets. My bar mitzvah was at an orthodox synagogue on . . . Darcy." (An orthodox synagogue is one that follows the established doctrine of Judaism.) His friendly manner and down-to-earth

Gehry stands in front of a model during the unveiling of his planned redesign for the Art Gallery of Ontario.

nature endeared him to a new generation of Canadians. On February 11, 2004, he officially laid out his plans for the museum.

Transformation AGO, to be completed in the fall of 2007, will include a titanium and glass exterior. An atrium open to natural light and a spiral staircase will provide a dramatic entrance to the museum. Glass walls and skylights will add to the feeling of openness throughout the interior. Gehry has also included a sculpture gallery and a new center for contemporary art that will face Grange Park. The third floor will feature a multipurpose area for special events.

More Honors

While designing the renovation of the AGO, the European Academy of Sciences and Arts honored Gehry for the contribution he has made in the field of architecture. The academy, composed of thirteen hundred scientists, researchers, philosophers, and artists, has the mission to contribute to the future of Europe and its unity by promoting knowledge, cooperation, and tolerance. Gehry was also named a Companion to the Order of Canada, which he considered a significant honor. It is Canada's highest honor given for lifetime achievement in one's field. The award recognizes people who have made a difference to Canada. Gehry has already received more than one hundred American Institute of Architects (AIA) awards.

Since 2004 Gehry has had the honor of serving on the jury of the Pritzker Architecture Prize, the prestigious prize he himself won in 1989. On March 21, 2004, it awarded the prize to Zaha Hadid, an Iraqi-born architect and the first woman to receive it. "[She] is probably one of the youngest laureates and has one of the clearest [directions] we've seen in many years," Gehry said. "Each project unfolds with new excitement and innovation." Hadid credited the opening of Gehry's unique Guggenheim Museum in Bilbao for generating greater interest in her own bold and innovative work.

Will Gehry's new buildings have the incredible effect on their communities that the Guggenheim has had on Bilbao? Only time will tell. Like new music and new art, new architecture often takes time to be understood and appreciated. Stravinsky's *Rite of Spring* and Brancusi's *Golden Fish* still baffle some people—and enchant many others.

As architecture critic Paul Goldberger explains: "There are those who will never respond to Gehry's work—who feel that his intensely romantic, emotional forms are self-indulgent—and those people are missing an architectural experience of immense power...."

Goldberger is among numerous critics who see a genius in Frank Gehry. Ada Louise Huxtable, the first architecture critic for the *New York Times* and recipient of the first Pulitzer Prize for Distinguished Criticism, summed up Gehry's special gifts to the world of architecture:

> Delight breaks through constantly; there are no gloomy Gehry buildings. One cannot think of anything he has done that does not make one smile.... These are light and lively designs and buildings that lift the spirit with revelations of how the seemingly ordinary can become extraordinary by acts of imagination.... He will continue... turning the practical into the lyrical, and architecture into art.

One of Gehry's biggest challenges may be the new performing arts center at Ground Zero, the site of the September 11, 2001, World Trade Center tragedy. Gehry said that "designing a building for dance and theater was what attracted him to the project." Gehry is one of several architects involved in designing the memorial site.

As he grows older, Gehry senses the shortness of time and the importance of being as productive as possible. With many projects in the planning stages—all over the world—Gehry is busier than ever. "I just want to do all that stuff," he says, "and play hockey too."

Gehry and his wife, Berta, pictured here at the opening of the Walt Disney Concert Hall, are planning a new home in Venice, California.

EPILOGUE

Twenty-five years after Gehry built his house in Santa Monica, California—the house that shocked the neighbors—he decided it was time for a change. The house had become a symbol, attracting daily visits from tourists and local residents. He wanted to free his family from the burden such intrusion put on their lives. His family's comfort was much more important to him than the public's attention. On January 9, 2005, his plans for a new home made headlines in the *New York Times*: "Frank Gehry Builds His California Dream House."

"I really agonized about how Berta and I wanted to live," Gehry told the *Times*. "I like to feel her presence sometimes even when I'm not standing next to her. But she needs her own world, too." Starting over in a new location—Venice, California—appealed to them both. The new house, a part of a compound (a few structures on the same lot), will be surrounded by trees and will feature screened porches that open out to gardens. The compound will cover three lots, providing smaller structures for the children, guest rooms, a gym, and a garage. A "living pavilion" will be used in a variety of ways—from a screening room for watching movies to a party room.

Gehry will use glass to "refract [change] images of trees and houses outside and of people moving around inside, like an indoor-outdoor hall of mirrors," writes journalist Nicolai Ouroussoff. In contrast, the private quarters for Frank and Berta will create a tree house feeling. "The whole design is set up so that you can break it back down into its individual lots," Gehry says. "So when we're gone, the kids can sell off parts of it... or get rid of the whole thing. It's really for them."

Gehry has made changes in his office headquarters as well as in his living quarters. The firm's headquarters is now located in Marina Del Rey—about twelve miles from downtown Los Angeles and only a few minutes away from the site of his new home. But even at the age of seventy-six, Gehry's energy and passion for his work remain unchanged.

TIMELINE

1929 Gehry was born on February 28, in Toronto, Canada.
1947 He moved with his family to Los Angeles.
1952 He married Anita Snyder.
1953–1961 Gehry apprenticed with Victor Gruen in Los Angeles and with André Remondet in Paris, France.
1954 He received a bachelor of architecture degree from the University of Southern California.
1956–1957 He studied city planning at Harvard University Graduate School of Design.
1962 He founded his architectural firm Frank O. Gehry & Associates in Los Angeles.
1968 He was divorced from Anita Snyder Gehry.
1972–1973 Gehry was assistant professor at the University of Southern California.
1974 He was elected to the College of Fellows at the American Institute of Architects.
1975 He married Berta Aguilera.
1976 He was a visiting critic at Rice University.
1977 Gehry received the Arnold W. Brunner Memorial Prize in Architecture from the American Academy adn Institue of Arts and Letters.
1977–1979 He was a visiting critic at the University of California.
1979 He held the William Bishop Chair at Yale University.
1982 He held the Charlotte Davenport Professorship in Architecture at Yale University. He held this position again in 1985 and 1987–1989.
1983 Gehry was a visiting critic at Harvard University.
1984 He was the Eliot Noyes Chair at Harvard University
1986 A retrospective exhibition of Gehry's work was held at the Walker Art Center, Minneapolis, and traveled to Atlanta, Houston, Toronto, Los Angeles, and New York.
1987 He was a Fellow of the American Academy and Institute of Arts and Letters
1989 He was an assistant professor at the Univeristy of Southern California.
He received the Pritzker Architecture Prize.
1991 Gehry was a trustee of the American Academy in Rome.
1992 He was a Fellow of the American Academy of Arts and Sciences.
1994 Gehry received the Wolf Prize in Art (Architecture) and the

Praemium Imperiale Award in Architecture by the Japan Art Association.

He received the Dorothy and Lillian Gish Award for Lifetime Contribution to the Arts.

1996 He received the title of Academician by the National Academy of Design.

1996–1997 He was a visiting scholar at the Federal Institute of Technology in Zurich, Switzerland.

1997 He received the Friedrich Kiesler Prize. He was an honorary consul of the city of Bilbao.

1998 He was an Honorary Academician at the Royal Academy of Arts and a visiting professor at the University of California. He recieved the gold medal at the Royal Architectural Institute of Canada.

1999 He received the American Institute of Architects gold medal for lifetime achievement.

2000 Gehry received the British Architects gold medal from the Royal Institute.

2004 He received the Royal Fine Art Commission's British Building of the Year award for Maggie's Centre in Dundee, Scotland.

Gehry was chosen to design the Performing Arts Center at Ground Zero in New York City.

Gehry visits the construction site of one of his buildings (the Massachusetts Institute of Technology (MIT) Stata Center) in 2004.

Selected Buildings by Frank Gehry

American Center, Paris, France
Cabrillo Marine Museum, Los Angeles, California
California Aerospace Museum, Los Angeles, California
Center for the Visual Arts, Toledo, Ohio
Edgemar Development, Santa Monica, California
Experience Music Project, Seattle, Washington
Fishdance Restaurant, Kobe, Japan
Frederick R. Weisman Art Museum, Minneapolis, Minnesota
Gehry House, Santa Monica, California
Goldwyn Branch Library, Hollywood, California
Guggenheim Museum Bilbao, Bilbao, Spain
Headquarters for the DG Bank, Berlin, Germany
Herman Miller Facilities, Rocklin, California
Hollywood Bowl, Hollywood, California
Jay Pritzker Pavilion, Millennium Park, Chicago, Illinois.
Joseph Magnin Store, Costa Mesa, California
Loyola Marymount University Law School, Los Angeles, California
Norton House, Venice, California
Office Building for Nationale-Nederlanden, Prague, Czech Republic
O'Neil Hay Barn, San Juan Capistrano, California
Ron Davis Studio and House, Malibu, California
Rouse Company Headquarters, Columbia, Maryland
Ruscha House, 29 Palms, California
Santa Monica Place, Santa Monica, California
Schnaubel Residence, Brentwood, California
Venice Beach House, Venice, California
Vitra Design Museum, Weil-am-Rheim, Germany
Vitra International Headquarters, Basel, Switzerland
Walt Disney Concert Hall, Los Angeles, California
Winton Guesthouse, Wayzata, Minnesota
Wosk Residence, Beverly Hills, California
Yale Psychiatric Institute, New Haven, Connecticut

Partial List of Buildings in Progress

Art Gallery of Ontario renovation, Toronto, Canada
Basketball Arena and Complex, Brooklyn, New York.
Marques de Riscal Winery expansion, El Ciego, Spain
Ohr-OKeefe Museums, Biloxi, Mississippi
Performing Arts Center, Bard College, Annandale-on-Hudson, New York
Peter B. Lewis Campus of the Weatherhead School of Management at Case Western Reserve University, Cleveland, Ohio

SOURCES

- 7 Paul Goldberger, "Good Vibrations," *The New Yorker*, September 29, 2003, 108.
- 8 Ibid.
- 9 Joseph Morgenstern, "The Gehry Style," *New York Times Magazine*, May 16, 1982, 58.
- 12 Ibid.
- 13 Doreen Nelson, in a telephone conversation with the author, March 8, 2004.
- 13–14 Morgenstern, 54.
- 14 Martin Knelman, "Native Son Gehry Recalls Boyhood," *Toronto Star*, January 26, 2004, A3.
- 16 Morgenstern, 58.
- 16 Ibid.
- 16–17 Doreen Nelson, in telephone conversation with the author, March 8, 2004.
- 17 Ibid.
- 20 Knelman, A4.
- 20 David Levy, "The Frank Gehry Experience," *Time Magazine*, June 26, 2000, 64.
- 23 Morgenstern, 48.
- 27–28 Ibid.
- 29 Ibid.
- 29 Ibid., 51.
- 32 Ibid.
- 35 Ibid., 62.
- 36 Ibid., 54.
- 37 Ibid., 64.
- 40 "Frank Gehry: Pritzker Architecture Prize Laureate, 1989." *Pritzker Prize*, http://www.pritzkerprize.com/gehry.htm (accessed March 25, 2005).
- 40–41 Penny Winton, in conversation with the author, March 1, 2004.
- 43 *Pritzker Prize*.
- 43 Ibid.
- 45 Goldberger, 108.

49 Morgenstern, 66.
49 *Pritzker Prize*.
49 Ibid.
50 Ibid.
50 Ibid.
50 Ibid.
51 Ibid.
53 Comments of unidentified University of Minnesota students in a Weisman Art Museum pamphlet (Minneapolis: University of Minnesota), n.d.
55 Lyndel King, interviewed by author, November 15, 2004.
55 Steen Estvad Petersen, "Jumbo Architecture," in *Frank O. Gehry: The Architect's Studio*, ed. Kirsten Degel (Humlebaek, Denmark: Louisiana Museum of Modern Art, 1998), 34.
59 Ibid.
61 Ibid., 36.
63 Doreen Nelson, in conversation with the author, March 8, 2004.
64 Petersen, 36.
64 Morgenstern, 66.
64 Ibid.
64–65 Ibid.
65 "Frank Gehry," *Contemporary Newsmakers 1987*, Gale Research, 1988. Detroit, 2004. http://galegroup.com/servlet/SRC.
66 Ibid.
70 Cathleen McGuigan, "A Mighty Monument to Music," *Newsweek*, August 18, 2003, 50.
70 Diane Haithman,"Disney Hall: The Opening," *Los Angeles Times*, October 19, 2003, E41.
71 Melissa Biggs Bradley, "Disney Hall Grand Opening," *Town & Country*, January, 2004, 138.
72 Mary McNamara, "Disney Hall: The Opening," *Los Angeles Times*, October 19, 2003, E38.
72 McGuigan, 50.
73–74 McNamara, E38.
75 Christopher Reynolds, "Disney Hall The Opening," *Los Angeles Times*, October 19, 2003, E46.
75 Ibid.

75 Ibid.
75 Ibid.
75 Ibid.
75 Ibid.
75 Janet Eastman, "Disney Hall: The Opening," *Los Angeles Times*, October 24, 2003, E1.
75 Ibid.
76 Christopher Knight, "Disney Hall: The Opening," *Los Angeles Times*, October 19, 2003, E46.
77 McGuigan, 50.
78 McNamara, E38.
79 Reynolds, E43.
81 "Frank Gehry: On to Ohr," *Smithsonian*, February 2004, 93.
82 Ibid.
82 Ibid., 94.
82 Ibid.
85 "Bring Basketball to Brooklyn!" *B-Ball*. http://www.bball.net (accessed March 25, 2005).
85–86 Ibid.
88 McGuigan, 50.
89 Ibid.
89 Knelman, A3.
91–92 Ibid.
92–93 Ibid.
94 Andrew Bridges, "For First Time, Woman Wins Top Honor in Architecture," Minneapolis *Star Tribune*, March 22, 2004, A9.
94 Goldberger, 108.
95 Ada Louise Huxtable, "On Awarding the Prize," *Pritzker Prize*, http://pritzkerprize.com/gehry.htm (accessed March 25, 2005).
95 Robin Pogrebin, "Gehry Is Chosen to Design Ground Zero Performance Center," *New York Times*, October 13, 2004, A27.
95 McGuigan, 50.
97 Nicolai Ouroussoff, "Frank Gehry Builds His California Dream House," *New York Times*, January 9, 2005, AR34.
98 Ibid.

Selected Bibliography

Books and Articles

Boehm, Mike. "Disney Hall: The Opening." *Los Angeles Times,* October 19, 2003, E41.

Bradley, Melissa Biggs. "Disney Hall Grand Opening." *Town & Country,* January 2004, 138.

Dal Co, Francesco, and Kurt W. Forster. *Frank O. Gehry: The Complete Works.* New York: The Monacelli Press, Inc., 1998.

Drobojowska, Hunter. "Fran Gehry's Grand Illusions." *Art News,* October 1998, 116–21.

Eastman, Janet. "Disney Hall: The Opening." *Los Angeles Times* October 24, 2003, E1.

Forster, Kurt W. *Frank O. Gehry: Guggenheim Bilbao Museo.* Stuttgart, Germany: Edition Axel Menges, 1998.

Frank O. Gehry: The Architect's Studio. Humlebaek, Denmark: Louisiana Museum of Modern Art, 1998.

Goldberger, Paul. "Good Vibrations." *New Yorker,* September 29, 2003, 108.

Ivy, Robert. "Frank Gehry: Plain Talk with a Master." *Architectural Record,* May 1999, 184–92, 356, 359–60.

Knelman, Martin. "Native Son Gehry Recalls Boyhood." *Toronto Star,* January 26, 2004, A3.

McGuigan, Cathleen. "A Mighty Monument to Music." *Newsweek,* August 18, 2003, 50.

McNamara, Mary. "Disney Hall: The Opening." *Los Angeles Times,* October 19, 2003, E38.

Miklosko, Helga. "Dancing House." *Architectural Record,* April 1997, 38–44.

Morgenstern, Joseph. "The Gehry Style." *New York Times Magazine,* May 16, 1982, 48–66.

Muschamp, Herbert. "In the Public Interest." *New York Times Magazine,* July 21, 1996, 38–41.

Ouroussoff, Nicolai. "Frank Gehry Builds His California Dream House." *New York Times,* January 9, 2005, AR34.

Petersen, Steen Estvad. "Jumbo Architecture." In *Frank O. Gehry: The Architect's Studio*, edited by Kirsten Degel. Humlebaek, Denmark: Louisiana Museum of Modern Art, 1998.

Pogrebin, Robin. "Gehry Is Chosen to Design Ground Zero Performance Center." *New York Times*, October 13, 2004, A27.

Ragheb, J. Fiona, ed. *Frank Gehry, Architect*. New York: Solomon R. Guggenheim Museum, 2001.

Sorkin, Michael, Mildred Friedman, et al., eds. *Gehry Talks*. New York: Rizzoli International Publications, 1999.

Steele, James. *California Aerospace Museum: Frank Gehry*. London: Phaidon Press, 1994.

Stephens, Suzanne. "The Bilbao Effect." *Architectural Record*, May 1999, 168–73.

Stung, Naomi. *Frank Gehry*. London: Carlton Books Limited, 2000.

Tomkin, Calvin. "The Maverick." *New Yorker*, June 7, 1997, 38–45.

WEBSITES

"Bring Basketball to Brooklyn." *B-Ball*. March 25, 2005. http://www.bball.net

"Frank Gehry: Pritzker Architecture Prize Laureate 1989," *Pritzker Prize*. March 25, 2005. http://www.pritzkerprize.com/gehry.htm

"Frank O. Gehry." *Contemporary Newsmakers 1987*. March 25, 2005. http://www.galegroup.com/servlet/SRC

"Transformation AGO-NEW BUILDING." *Art Gallery of Ontario*. http://www.ago.net/trandsformatiuon/gehry.inc.cfm

FURTHER READING AND WEBSITES

BOOKS

The Building: Weisman Art Museum. Minneapolis: University of Minnesota, 2003.

Chollet, Laurence. *The Essential Frank O. Gehry.* New York: Abrams, 2001.

Greenberg, Jan, and Sandra Jordan. *Frank O. Gehry Outside In.* New York: Dorling Kindersley Publishing, Inc., 2000.

WEBSITES

Archpedia.
http://www.archpedia.com
On this website, readers will find biographical information, interviews, and photos of works designed by Frank Gehry.

B-Ball.
http://www.bball.net
Information about Gehry's vision for a world-class basketball arena and multiuse complex in Brooklyn, New York, is fully discussed on this site.

Contemporary Newsmakers 1987. "Frank O. Gehry."
http://www.galegroup.com/servlet/SRC
This site is a student resource center for learning facts about Frank Gehry's life.

Salon.com. "Frank Gehry."
http://www.salon.com/people/bc/1999/10/05/gehry/print.html
A discussion of the Guggenheim Museum in Bilbao, the differences between Gehry's work and that of other renowned architects, and Gehry's creative use of a variety of materials are some of the topics covered here.

INDEX

anti-Semitism, 8, 14, 15, 20
architectural contributions, designs, and projects: Art Gallery of Ontario (AGO), 91–93, Arts Park, 41; Brooklyn Atlantic Yards, 85–86; Cabrillo Marine Museum, 35–37; California Aerospace Museum, 40, 101; Chiat/Day Office, 43, 45; Experience Music Project, 62, 64–66, 67, 69; Fish sculpture, 46–49; Frederick R. Weisman Art Museum, 52, 53–55, 59, 60; Guggenheim Museums (Bilbao and New York City), 8, 56–57, 58–59, 61, 86, 94; Los Angeles Children's Museum, 41; Los Angeles County Museum of Art, 38, 39–40; Loyola Marymount University, 30–31; Maggie's Centre, 67, 100; Notre-Dame-du-Haut, 22; Ohr-O'Keefe Museums, 81–82; Olympics, the, 47–49, 51, 58; O'Neil Hay Barn, 23; performing arts center at Ground Zero, New York City, 95; Walker Art Center, 12, 46; Walt Disney Concert Hall, 6, 7–8, 68, 71–79, 96, 101: design challenges: 71–77; Winton Guesthouse, 40–43
architectural materials, 13; chain link fence, 35–37; Colorcore (laminate), 46; glass, 13, 32, 46, 66–67, 93, 97–98; titanium, 59, 61, 88, 93; wood, 13, 72
architectural models: computer generated, 48, 51, 56, 58–59; wood and foam, 57, 65
awards, honors, and prizes, 92, 93–95; Architect of the Year, 32; Arnold W. Brunner Prize, 40, 99; Companion to the Order of Canada, 93–94; Friedrich Kiesler Prize, 64; Pritzker Architecture Prize, 49–51; Royal Fine Art Commission's British Building of the Year, 67, 100

building projects. *See* architectural contributions, designs, and projects

computer aided three-dimensional interactive application (CATIA). *See* architectural models
creative influences, 21; art, music, and sculpture: 8, 13, 14, 20, 21, 22, 39–40, 44, 76–77, 94; Brancusi,

Constantin, 43, 44, 94;
Caplan's Hardware, 13; Le
Corbusier, 21, 22–23; Greco-
Roman, 31–35; Johnson,
Philip, 21, 27, 27;
Oldenburg, Claes, 43, 45;
Wright, Frank Lloyd, 21

Disney, Lillian, 7, 69–71, 72
Disney, Walt, 7, 69

Gehry, Alejandro (son), 25,
  29–30, 65–66
Gehry, Anita Snyder (wife),
  20, 23–24, 99
Gehry, Berta Aguilera (wife),
  25, 28–30, 88–89, 96, 97, 98,
  99
Gehry, Brina (daughter), 20,
  64
Gehry (Goldberg), Frank
  Owen: birth and childhood,
  11–12: early creative
  adventures, 13–16; birth
  name, 11; and collaboration
  and teaching, 41, 43, 45, 49,
  76, 77, 86; 88–89; furniture
  design, 23–25; at Harvard
  Graduate School of Design,
  21; in high school, 14–15,
  16; marriage and divorce,
  20, 23, 25; military service,
  21; and Santa Monica,
  California, home, 26, 97–98;
  selected buildings and
  buildings in progress,
  101–102; at University of
  Southern California (USC),
  19–21; writings, 61

Gehry, Leslie (daughter), 20, 64
Gehry, Samuel (son), 25, 28,
  64–65
Gehry and Associates, Frank
  O., 86, 88–89
Gehry Design, 86–87
Gehry Partners, 57, 86–87
Gehry Technologies, 86–87, 88
Goldberg, Irving (father),
  12–13, 15, 16
Goldberg, Lillian Caplan
  (mother), 11–12
Goldberg, Sam (grandfather),
  11
Goldberg, Thelma (mother),
  13, 16, 63
Gruen Associates, Victor,
  20–21, 23

Judaism, 8, 10, 11–12, 15, 20.
  See also anti-Semitism

Mies Van Der Rohe, Ludwig,
  21
Miller, Diane Disney, 69–70, 71

Nelson, Doreen, 13, 16–17,
  41, 63

Ohr, George, 81–84
O'Keefe, Jeremiah, 81, 82

Salonen, Esa Pekka, 77, 78
Shulman, Julius, 76

Toyota, Yasuhisa, 77, 78

Winton, David and Penny,
  40–42

OTHER TITLES FROM LERNER AND A&E®:

Arnold Schwarzenegger
Ariel Sharon
Arthur Ashe
The Beatles
Benito Mussolini
Benjamin Franklin
Bill Gates
Bruce Lee
Carl Sagan
Chief Crazy Horse
Christopher Reeve
Colin Powell
Daring Pirate Women
Edgar Allan Poe
Eleanor Roosevelt
Fidel Castro
George Lucas
George W. Bush
Gloria Estefan
Hillary Rodham Clinton
Jack London
Jacques Cousteau
Jane Austen
Jesse Owens
Jesse Ventura
Jimi Hendrix
J. K. Rowling
John Glenn
Latin Sensations

Legends of Dracula
Legends of Santa Claus
Louisa May Alcott
Madeleine Albright
Malcolm X
Mark Twain
Maya Angelou
Mohandas Gandhi
Mother Teresa
Nelson Mandela
Oprah Winfrey
Osama bin Laden
Pope John Paul II
Princess Diana
Queen Cleopatra
Queen Elizabeth I
Queen Latifah
Rosie O'Donnell
Saddam Hussein
Saint Joan of Arc
Thurgood Marshall
Tiger Woods
Tony Blair
Vladimir Putin
William Shakespeare
Wilma Rudolph
Women in Space
Women of the Wild West
Yasser Arafat

About the Author

Caroline Evensen Lazo has written numerous biographies. *Alice Walker: Freedom Writer*, a Society of School Librarians International (SSLI) Honor Book, and *Arthur Ashe* were selected as Notable Social Studies Trade Books for Young People by the National Council for Social Studies. Her other works include *F. Scott Fitzgerald*, *Gloria Steinem*, *Leonard Bernstein*, and *Harry S. Truman*.

Photo Acknowledgments

The images in this book are used with permission of: © Carlo Allegri/Getty Images for LAPA, p. 2; © Armando Arorizo/ZUMA Press, p. 4; © Nathan Benn/CORBIS, p. 10; © Frank Gehry, Standing Glass Fish, 1986, wood, glass, steel, silicone, plexiglass, rubber, 264 x 168 x 102"/Collection Walker Art Center, Minneapolis/Gift of Anne Pierce Rogers in honor of her grandchildren, Anne and Will Rogers and Lily Rogers Grant, 1986/photo by Sam Lund/Independent Picture Service, p. 12; © Erin Combs/Toronto Star/ZUMA Press, p. 14; © William Boyce/CORBIS, p. 18; © Nina Leen/Time Life Pictures/Getty Images, p. 21; © Owen Franken/CORBIS, p. 22; © Gehry Partners, LLP, pp. 24, 26, 36, 38, 45, 57, 59, 71, 73, 74, 80, 87, 88; © John Kreul/Independent Picture Service, p. 28; © A.A.M. Van der Heyden/Independent Picture Service, p. 31; © Roger Ressmeyer/CORBIS, pp. 33, 34; © Penny and David Winton, p. 42; © Eliot Elisofon/Time Life Pictures/Getty Images, p. 44; © Edifice/CORBIS, p. 47; © Douglas Kirkland/CORBIS, p. 48; © Sam Lund /Independent Picture Service, p. 52; Lyndel King, pp. 54, 66; © Jose Fuste Raga/CORBIS, p. 60; © Richard Cummins/CORBIS, p. 62; © Ted Soqui/CORBIS, p. 68; © AP | Wide World Photos, pp. 78, 86, 92, 96; Just Art Pottery, p. 83; © Gala/SuperStock, p. 90; © Richard Sobol/ZUMA Press, p. 100. Front cover: © TOUHIG SION/CORBIS SYGMA. Back cover: © Sam Lund/Independent Picture Service

Websites

Website addresses in this book were valid at the time of printing. However, because of the nature of the Internet, some addresses may have changed or sites may have closed since publication. While the author and Publisher regret any inconvenience this may cause readers, no responsibility for any such changes can be accepted by the author or Publisher.